Finley Flowers

Art-Rageous

BY JESSICA YOUNG

ILLUSTRATED BY JESSICA SECHERET

PICTURE WINDOW BOOKS
a capstone imprint

Finley Flowers is published by Picture Window Books
A Capstone Imprint
1710 Roe Crest Drive
North Mankato, MN 56003
www.mycapstone.com

Library of Congress Cataloging-in-Publication Data
Young, Jessica (Jessica E.), author.
  Art-rageous / by Jessica Young ; illustrations by Jessica
Secheret.
     pages cm. -- (Finley Flowers)

Summary: After a class field trip to the art museum,
fourth graders Finley, Henry, and Olivia are assigned a
project that is supposed to define art, which is difficult,
because they all liked very different paintings — but for
their group project they come up with a presentation that
captures their combined vision.

ISBN: 978-1-4795-6177-3 (hardcover) -- 978-1-4795-5960-2
(paper over board) -- 978-1-4795-9780-2 (paperback)
978-1-4795-6188-9 (eBook PDF) -- 9781-4795-8591-5
(reflowable epub)

1. Art museums--Juvenile fiction. 2. School field trips--
Juvenile fiction. 3. Aesthetics--Juvenile fiction. 4. Middle-
born children--Juvenile fiction. 5. Families--Juvenile
fiction. 6. Friendship--Juvenile fiction. 7. Elementary
schools--Juvenile fiction. [1. Art--Fiction. 2. School field
trips--Fiction. 3. Middle-born children--Fiction. 4. Family
life--Fiction. 5. Friendship--Fiction. 6. Schools--Fiction.] I.
Secheret, Jessica, illustrator. II. Title.

PZ7.Y8657Ar 2015
813.6--dc23
 [Fic]

                          2014046195

Editor: Alison Deering
Designer: Kristi Carlson

Vector Images: Shutterstock

Printed in the United States of America.
009737F16

For Omi, who loved all kinds of art

TABLE OF CONTENTS

Chapter 1
FEELING FALL-ISH

Finley Flowers was running late. Mom had lost her keys again, and Finley's little sister, Evie, had taken forever to eat breakfast. When Mom dropped Finley and Evie off at school, Finley's best friend, Henry Lin, was waiting on the front steps.

"Earth to Finley! Hurry up!" Henry called as Evie skipped past him into the building.

Finley jumped for a leaf dangling from a branch and missed. "It's too nice to go inside! Fall's my favorite season — look, the trees are on fire!"

Henry glanced at his watch and made a beeline for the school doors. "We only have two minutes until class starts! Let's go!"

Finley and Henry got to their classroom just before the bell rang. Ms. Bird, their teacher, was waiting at the door. "Good morning, you two," she said in her chirpy morning voice. "You can unpack your things, but leave your jackets on — we'll be going right back outside."

"Woo-hoo!" Finley cheered. Fourth grade was the best! She might not get perfect grades like her older brother, Zack, but she loved school. Ms. Bird was always full of fun surprises.

Finley put away her books and peeked inside her lunchbox. Mom had packed a cucumber and cream cheese sandwich again. Evie's favorite — *not* Finley's.

Grrr, Finley thought. *I'm going to have to start making my own lunch.*

Once Ms. Bird had taken attendance, the class lined
up at the door. Finley got a spot near the front. She
could barely wait to find out where they were going.
She was so hoppity, she felt like she was about to pop.

"What are we going to do?" Henry asked.

"We're going on a treasure hunt," Ms. Bird said with a mysterious look.

"Ahoy, me hearties!" Henry said in his best pirate accent. "We're off to search for treasure!"

Ms. Bird smiled. "Aye, Henry! Hopefully, we won't have to search too far."

Ms. Bird led the class outside and had them form a circle under a huge oak tree. "Today we're going to start a new unit of study," she explained. "We'll be looking at art, talking about art, and making art. On Monday we'll take our field trip downtown to the new art museum for some inspiration."

Finley lit up. *Finally!* she thought. She'd been waiting for the field trip for weeks. When Ms. Bird had passed out the permission slips, Finley had insisted that Mom sign hers right away.

The art museum was the perfect field trip for Finley. She'd considered being an inventor when she grew up, but being an artist was even better! After all, artists were kind of like inventors. They were always coming up with new things and being famous for making stuff. It was the ideal job for her — she had a million ideas, and she made stuff all the time!

"This morning, we'll warm up with an art activity," Ms. Bird continued. "Part one is a treasure hunt for fall leaves. Try to collect lots of interesting shapes and colors. You have ten minutes. Ready . . . go!"

Students scattered in all directions, darting from leaf to leaf like bees to flowers. Finley spotted a bright-yellow leaf and raced toward it. Olivia Snotham zoomed in and reached down to grab the same one, but Finley got there first.

"Aw!" Olivia pouted. "I wanted that one!"

"Here," Finley said, holding it out by the stem. "There are lots more."

"Thanks." Olivia took the leaf and held it up to the light.

Finley looked around, then plucked up a purple-ish-brown-ish one and a brilliant orange one. Her friends Kate and Lia ran past, scooping up handfuls of leaves and stuffing them into their pockets. A red maple leaf streaked by, and Finley lunged for it, colliding with Henry.

"Sorry!" they said together.

Henry laughed. "Whatcha got?"

Finley fanned out her leaves for him to see.

"Nice!" Henry said. "Look at this." He held out a yellow one tinged with rusty orange.

"Cool! Ooh, look — a lime-green one!" Finley said, pointing across the lawn. Then she dashed off to claim it for her collection.

Just as Finley had picked her tenth leaf, Ms. Bird rang the chime. "Everyone line up!" she called. "Bring your treasures with you — it's time for part two!"

Finley squeezed in line behind Kate and Lia and followed the rest of the students inside. When they got back to the classroom, Ms. Bird opened the cupboard and set some art supplies on the back counter.

Finley couldn't wait to get started. She had never met an art material she didn't like. She liked the waxy, sweet smell of the crayons and the chalky softness of the pastels. She liked the silky-tipped watercolor brushes and the flat-bristled ones they used with thick tempera paint. Pencils, glue, clay, tissue paper — Finley loved them all!

Henry looked at Finley and grinned. "Turn on your Flower Power!" That was his nickname for the idea garden in her head where all her Fin-teresting thoughts grew.

Finley took her seat and arranged the leaves on her desk. There were three bumpy-edged oak leaves, two of the football-shaped purple-ish ones, three golden-brown ones with zig-zaggy edges, the lime-green one, and four so orange they looked like they'd glow in the dark.

Finley wondered what the assignment would be.

Who knows? she thought. *Maybe I'll make something so amazingly Fin-tastic they'll put it in a museum! This could be the start of something big!*

Chapter 2
WHIRLY, TWIRLY GIRL

Once everyone was seated, Ms. Bird walked up and down the rows, passing out sheets of big white paper and packs of colored pencils. "We're going to use the leaves we've collected to make leaf drawings," she explained. "Study them. Remember what the trees looked like, and try to capture the season of fall on paper."

Finley closed her eyes and pictured the falling leaves. She'd seen reds, greens, yellows, purples, and oranges. They'd made her feel whirly. Twirly. Fall-ish.

Maybe her drawing could make someone else feel fall-ish, too.

Ms. Bird put on some no-words music. "This piece by the composer Vivaldi is about fall," she said. "It might help get you in the mood."

As the violins started their stately melody, Finley picked up a bunch of colored pencils. The music swelled, and Finley moved her hand in big arcs and swirls, like leaves fluttering in the breeze. She imagined the wind blowing right through her pencils, coming out on her paper in wavy lines.

Finley was in the middle of a leaf whirlwind when Olivia stopped by her desk on her way to the pencil sharpener. Olivia looked at Finley's drawing and scrunched up her nose. "That doesn't look *anything* like fall," she said. "Fall is pretty."

Finley stopped drawing. Suddenly she didn't feel so fall-ish anymore. At camp last summer, she and Olivia had started to become friends, but sometimes

Olivia still said things in a not-so-nice way. Finley looked down at her paper and frowned.

"I just mean I've seen you draw better than that," Olivia added. "That looks like . . . scribbles."

Finley felt her cheeks turn red. "Well, they're *my* scribbles," she said. "And *I* like them."

Olivia shrugged and went to sharpen her pencils.

Finley studied her drawing again. *She* thought it was pretty. But pretty was in the eye of the beholder. She'd learned that last year when she bedazzled the mailbox. It had taken her hours to glue on all those jewels, and Mom and Dad hadn't appreciated her hard work.

It's just like Grandma always said, Finley thought. *You can't please everyone all the time.*

Finley decided to ignore Olivia and went right back to swirling. When she finished her drawing, she stepped back to get a better view.

Who cares about pretty anyway? she thought. *My art is interesting and fun!*

"All right, class," said Ms. Bird. "Time to line up for recess!"

As Finley pushed in her chair, Henry held up his drawing for her to see. In the middle of the paper was a small, lone leaf. It had been carefully outlined and colored in layers of red, orange, and gold. "I only had time for one," he explained.

"Wow!" Finley said. "It looks just like a real leaf!"

"Thanks," said Henry. "I tried to draw lots of details. Let's see yours."

Finley unrolled her drawing and held it up. Henry studied it with his hard-thinking face. "Um, no offense," he said, "but that does not look like a real leaf."

"It's not a leaf, exactly," Finley explained. "It's how a leaf *feels.*"

Henry crinkled his forehead. "I don't get it," he said. "Leaves don't have feelings."

Finley laughed. "How do you know?" She put her drawing on Henry's desk and grabbed him by the arm. "Here," she said. "I'll show you."

They followed the rest of their classmates outside for recess, and Finley led Henry to the field by the playground. Then she took both of his hands in hers, leaned back, and spun around.

And around.

And around.

"This is how a leaf feels when it's blowing in the wind!" Finley shrieked. "All whirly and twirly!"

"Okay, okay!" Henry said, laughing. "Stop the ride! I get it!"

They tumbled onto the grass and watched the leaves spiral down.

"It's amazing how bright they are," Henry said, pointing. "They sure put on a show."

Finley grinned. *I'm going to put on a show, too!* she decided. *I'm going to be an artist and make my mark!*

Chapter 3
ART-SMART

Finley thought about the field trip all weekend. On Monday morning, she got up early and put on her artsy-est clothes: a red dress, yellow sweater, green tights, purple hairband, and sparkly blue shoes.

Perfect! she thought, checking her outfit in the mirror. *I look like a rainbow!*

Finley tucked her sketchbook and pencils into her backpack and bounded downstairs. Zack was already in the kitchen, sitting down to eat the last bagel.

"What's with the outfit?" he asked, shielding his eyes. "It's giving me a headache."

"Today's my class field trip to the art museum!" Finley announced. She grabbed some fruit salad out of the fridge and started arranging it into a colorful pattern on her plate. "We're getting inspiration for a special project."

Zack smeared more cream cheese on his bagel and took a big bite. "So?" he said, spraying crumbs as he spoke.

"*So,*" said Finley, "it's exciting, and I'm dressing for the occasion. I make art all the time, but I've never seen real, famous art in person!"

"Your Popsicle-stick pyramids and tinfoil tiaras aren't exactly art," Zack said. He crammed the rest of his bagel into his mouth, grabbed his backpack, and headed to catch the bus. "I hope they let you in dressed like that. There might be a rule about not clashing with the exhibit."

Finley made a face behind Zack's back. Just because he was in sixth grade now, he thought he knew everything. Finley might not get straight As like he did, but she was art-smart — and this was her chance to shine!

When Finley turned around, Evie was sitting at the kitchen table. "Cool shoes," Evie said, pointing to Finley's feet. "Can I borrow them?"

"No."

Evie pouted. "Why not?"

"Because I'm wearing them," Finley said, pouring herself some cereal. "Besides, they wouldn't fit you."

"What about that hairband?" Evie asked, chomping on her toast.

Finley shook her head. "I'm using it right now. Maybe another time."

"Yes!" Evie clapped her hands together. "I'll wear it tomorrow with my new jeans! I love sharing!"

Finley sighed. *Of course you do,* she thought. *You're always the share-ee, and I'm the share-er.*

Sometimes Finley wished she could trade Evie in for a big sister instead — someone who'd have cool stuff *she* could borrow. But Mom and Dad would never go for that. Evie was seven, but she'd always be their baby. And Zack would always be the oldest — he got to do everything first, and he did everything perfectly. Finley was stuck in the middle of the sibling sandwich, and she was starting to feel squished.

Finley was finishing off her cereal when Mom swooped through the kitchen with her briefcase in one hand and her coffee in the other. Before Finley could remind her of the field trip, Mom had breezed out the back door. "In the car, girls!" she called over her shoulder. "Come on, or we'll be late!"

No! Finley thought. *Not today!* She grabbed her backpack and jacket and stopped to help Evie put her shoes on. Evie could do it herself — she just took forever, and she refused to wear Velcro.

Her little sister stuck out one foot and then the other, and Finley tied her laces. Then Evie bounded out the door.

"Thanks for being ready to go, big girl!" Mom said as Evie climbed into her booster seat.

Finley scowled. *It's not fair,* she thought. *I'm pretty much Evie's personal assistant, but she gets all the credit.* Finley looked down at her sparkly shoes. *And Mom didn't even notice my outfit.*

Lately, Finley wondered if anyone noticed her at all. Between all of Zack's sports practices and games and Evie's play dates, it didn't seem like there was much time left for her. But that was about to change.

Soon I'll be a famous artist, Finley thought. *Not just Finley-in-the-middle.*

Chapter 4
INVENTION #5

When Finley got to her classroom, she spotted Olivia sitting in the reading corner, doodling in a black sketchbook. She was dressed all in black — from her boots to the ribbon in her hair.

"You look . . . interesting," Olivia said as Finley headed for the bookshelves. "Why all the crazy colors?"

"I'm dressed for the art museum." Finley told her. "Why all the black? Are you trying to be a ninja?"

Olivia rolled her eyes. "No, *I'm* dressed for the art museum. Real artists wear black."

Finley looked down at her green tights and sparkly blue shoes. "How do *you* know what real artists wear?" she asked, frowning.

Just then Henry bounded over. "Whoa!" he said to Finley. "You look like a party!" He glanced at Olivia. "And *you* look like a ninja."

Ms. Bird walked to the front of the class and rang her chime. "Please sit down and clear your desks," she said. "The bus is waiting to take us on our museum adventure!" When everyone was seated, she took attendance, then started calling students to line up. Henry and Kate's row was first.

"I'll save you a seat," Henry whispered to Finley as he pushed in his chair.

Finley's row was last. Before Ms. Bird had finished calling her name, Finley sprang out of her chair to take her place in line. She checked her backpack for her sketchbook and pencils, then followed the class out the door.

As Finley boarded the bus, Henry waved her over. "Window seat?" he said, standing so she could squeeze in. "I tried to get one close to the front."

"Thanks." Finley plunked her bag down and slid the window open. She was already feeling bus-sick. Short trips were sometimes okay, but after about fifteen minutes on a bus, her stomach always felt like she was on a roller coaster.

"Hope it's not a bumpy ride," Olivia piped up from behind them. "Remember last year's field trip to the pumpkin patch? Someone had a little tummy trouble."

"Let's not bring it up," said Henry. "Get it — *bring it up*?"

"Yuck." Olivia wrinkled her nose. "I've never thrown up in my whole life. Mom says I have an extra-strong stomach."

Good for you, Finley thought, as she leaned her forehead against the cool window.

The ride to the art museum was loud and long. Henry read his *Weird and Wacky Bugs* book, and Olivia doodled in her sketchbook. Finley wished she could draw too, but even the idea of it made her stomach do backflips.

As they wove through downtown traffic, the skyscrapers got taller. Suddenly, the bus lurched to a stop in front of a massive stone building, and the doors opened with a wheeze. Students jostled down the aisle and spilled out onto the sidewalk.

Finley stepped into the fresh, crisp air. "Close one," she said, making a face.

"I could tell," said Henry. "You were getting as green as your tights."

"Ha." Finley turned to study the building. Part of it was modern and sleek, and part of it was like a castle, with turrets and tall, pointy-arched windows.

A real museum! she thought. *The place where art lives!* She felt better already. She could hardly wait to get inside.

The students followed Ms. Bird up the front steps of the museum, then filed through a set of heavy, glass doors into an entryway with giant columns.

"Wow," said Henry, looking up at the vaulted ceiling. "This place is huge."

Ms. Bird led them down a long hall. Chattering voices and squeaking shoes echoed off the marble-tiled walls.

Peering through an arched doorway, Finley noticed a canvas covered with splashes and streaks of paint. The colors looked like they were playing tag. They made her want to jump in and play, too.

I bet the artist had fun making that, thought Finley. *And now it's hanging in the museum. One day my art will be hanging here!*

The class turned down a smaller corridor and passed a row of landscape paintings in fancy gold and silver frames.

Finley could only dream of having her artwork displayed like that. Lately, there was barely enough room for *her* drawings on the fridge. They were always half-covered by Zack's soccer schedules and Evie's sticker-studded worksheets.

The class hurried on like a line of ants. Ms. Bird turned through an archway and stopped in an enormous room full of paintings. "Before we get started, I'm going to divide you into small groups so you can explore the gallery. When you're finished we'll move on to the next exhibit as a class."

Finley crossed her fingers. *Henry, Henry, Henry,* she thought.

Ms. Bird went around the room, splitting the students up into groups. Finally, she pointed to Finley, Henry, and Olivia. "You three," she said. "You're a group."

Yes! Finley thought. *It worked!*

Henry grinned and gave Finley a thumbs-up sign.

"Here's your first mission," Ms. Bird said to the class. "Observe the art and pick your group's favorite piece. Then take notes and do some sketches to help you remember what it looks like. There will be a homework assignment and a group art project based on what you see today. As part of the group project, which is due on Thursday," Ms. Bird continued, "you'll be answering a very big question: what is art?"

Finley looked around. *That'll be easy,* she thought. *Art is everywhere!*

"Okay, team," Henry said. "Let's go find a favorite!"

Finley, Henry, and Olivia toured the gallery. Henry read the plaques on the wall and carefully copied down names and dates. Henry loved lists.

Olivia stood in front of each piece of art, crossed her arms, and glared at it like she was having a staring contest. Then she opened her sketchbook, put

Claude Monet, 1840-1926

Alfred Sisley, 1839-1899

Berthe Morisot, 1841-1895

Pierre-Auguste Renoir, 1841-1919

Suzanne Valadon, 1865-1938

Edgar Degas, 1834-1917

Vincent van Gogh, 1853-1890

Mary Cassatt, 1844-1926

on her serious face, and took some serious notes.

Finley didn't believe in reading plaques or taking notes. She had her own way of observing. First she looked at the pieces from far away, then up close. She looked at them with one eye, then the other. She focused her eyes, then made them go blurry. She even leaned way over and looked at them upside down.

"What are you doing?" Henry asked, walking up behind her. "Yoga?"

"It's my special way of looking at art," Finley told him. "You should try it."

Henry bent forward, trying to copy her pose. "Ugh," he said. "It makes me dizzy."

At the far end of the gallery, Finley, Henry, and Olivia came to a painting of a girl sitting under an apple tree. As Finley studied the painting, she could almost feel the warm breeze and smell the fresh, grassy scent of summer. When she moved in close, the girl vanished and became rough patches of color. When she stepped back, the patches blended together, and the girl reappeared as if by magic.

"What about this one?" Henry suggested as he copied down facts from the plaque. "I like it the best. It looks so real. I feel like I could walk right into it."

"Those aren't exactly my colors," said Olivia. "There's no purple."

As they rounded the corner into the next room, Finley spotted the painting she'd noticed on the way in — the one with the playful splashes and streaks. "Those are *my* colors!" she said, pointing. "That's definitely my favorite."

Finley, Olivia, and Henry stood in front of the huge canvas. All the bright colors made Finley feel like dancing. She wished she could bottle up its squiggly lines and splooshy shapes and take them with her for when she was feeling droopy.

"It's called *Invention #5*," said Henry. "It reminds me of your whirly-twirly leaf picture."

"It doesn't look like anything." Olivia pointed across the room to a portrait of an important-looking man on a horse. The background was dark and dreary, and the man looked like he'd lost his hamster. "That's *real* art."

Real boring, thought Finley. *That belongs in a snooze-eum.*

"They both must be art," she told Olivia. "Or they wouldn't be in an *art* museum."

Finley turned back to *Invention #5*. When she studied the splatters and drips, it was almost like she was right there, watching the artist work.

It would be pretty cool to make your mark on the world by making marks, she thought. *Maybe if I look closely, I'll learn how.*

Chapter 5
FOOD FOR THOUGHT

Finley opened her sketchbook and started to draw. She looked up, then down, up, then down, trying to match her lines to what she saw. It was hard to copy the colors with a plain old pencil, but she tried to imagine them as different shades of gray.

As Finley put the finishing touches on her sketch, Ms. Bird strolled by and rang her chime softly. "Come with me, friends," she said. "Time for something completely different." She disappeared through a nearby doorway, and the class followed.

The next gallery was smaller than the first one, but every wall was covered with paintings of bowls of fruit and vases of flowers.

"Weird," Henry said, glancing around. "It's a room full of fruit."

Finley studied the piece next to her. It showed a blue-and-white ceramic bowl full of apples, peaches, pears, and grapes. Next to it, on a rumpled tablecloth, a cantaloupe was cut open, exposing its gooey insides. Hunks of cheese and bread were arranged on a cutting board, which sat beside a pitcher full of nodding sunflowers.

"Now I'm craving a snack!" said Henry. "Although that bread would be pretty stale. These paintings are hundreds of years old." He started copying names and dates into his notebook.

"I finally found *my* favorite," said Olivia, pointing to a painting of pink and purple flowers. "That would go perfectly in my room — it matches my bedspread."

Finley didn't care much about matching. Matching wasn't interesting. As she studied the piece next to her, she noticed something strange. In the middle of the food was a gold pocket watch. "That's funny," she said. "Someone forgot their watch."

"Hey," said Henry. "That painting has one, too. And the one over there has an hourglass."

"What's that?" Finley asked, pointing to the painting behind Olivia.

Olivia made a face. "Ew — a cockroach!"

"Actually, it's a beetle," Henry said, moving in closer to study it. "It looks real, but it's just painted."

"Yikes! Look at *that* painting!" Finley blurted out. "There's a skull — right in the middle of the food!"

Just then Ms. Bird rang her chime. "All right, class," she said. "Observe these still-life paintings carefully. What do you see?"

"Lunch?" Henry said with a hopeful grin.

Ms. Bird smiled. "Yes, fruits and cheeses and bread — and some other objects from daily life. What else?"

Olivia put up her hand. "Why does that one have a skull?"

"Maybe it's a *skull*-pture," Henry whispered to Finley. Finley giggled.

"Good question, Olivia." Ms. Bird pointed to the next painting over. "This one is also a still life. No skull here, but look." She pointed to the pocket watch lying in the folds of the tablecloth. "How is the watch similar to the skull? Or the half-burned candles in this one? Or the bubbles in that one? What do all of these objects tell us?"

"I don't know," said Olivia. "But it seems kind of useless to have a skull at a picnic. Not to mention gross."

"Why didn't the artist just put *living* people at the picnic?" Finley asked. "A skull can't even eat."

Ms. Bird nodded. "Unfortunately, it's too late for him — or her — to enjoy all that food. But it's not too late for us." She looked at Finley and raised her eyebrows. "Food for thought."

Suddenly Henry's stomach growled. "Sorry," he said. "I need some food for *eating*!"

Ms. Bird laughed. "Then let's go get some lunch. Follow me."

As the class funneled out the doors, they passed some writing on the wall that read, *"Ars longa, vita brevis. (Art is long, life is short.)"*

Finley wasn't sure exactly what that meant, or what those still-life paintings were about, but she did know they definitely weren't her style. When she made *her* marks, they'd be big and messy, like the splashes and splotches of *Invention #5*. They'd be bright and happy and impossible to ignore!

As the class filed down the corridor, Finley heard noises coming from a room to their right. Ms. Bird paused, then ushered them into a darkened theater where a video was playing. The man in the video was wearing big rubber boots and wading in a stream, breaking up branches and arranging them to form a giant nest that jutted out over the rushing water. In the next part of the video, he was standing in the middle of a green field, stacking rocks into a humungous egg-shaped tower. After that, he was kneeling on a beach beside the ocean, gluing icicles together with water to make a spiky, frozen star.

"What in the world is he doing?" whispered Olivia.

"Art?" Finley whispered back.

"I don't get it," said Henry. "What's the point?"

"Maybe he likes making things outside," Finley whispered. "Or maybe he's just having fun experimenting."

Ms. Bird gestured for the class to follow her and slipped out the back of the theater. "That art by Andy Goldsworthy was interesting," she said as they headed toward the museum café. "It was different from the other things we saw today — more like a whole art experience."

"I can't wait to experience the café," Henry said, fishing out his lunch money. "Those still-life paintings made me hungry."

Finley studied the menu as they waited in line. "I don't know what to get," she said. "The salads look good. But fall is soup season."

"You can't go wrong with cheese pizza," said Olivia.

Eventually Finley decided on potato soup and salad with a cranberry-oatmeal cookie for dessert. Henry ordered French toast with a side of French fries. "To go with all those French paintings," he explained.

Finley, Henry, and Olivia paid for their food and carried their trays to one of the marble-topped café tables. Henry drizzled syrup over his French toast and squirted his fries with ketchup. "So what's our favorite piece?" he asked.

"Definitely the vase of flowers," said Olivia, cutting her pizza into bite-sized pieces. "It was beautiful."

"I vote for *Invention #5* — the one with all the bright colors," said Finley. "I like that they're not

trying to be a person or place or thing. They're just being themselves."

"My favorite's still the portrait of the girl," said Henry. "She looked so real!"

"Well, *I'm* not going to change my mind," said Olivia. "I like what I like."

"We *all* like what we like," Finley said. "But we're supposed to pick *one* piece, not three."

"It looks like we have a problem," said Henry.

Finley frowned. "At least that's one thing we all agree on."

Chapter 6

GROUP WORK, SHMOOP WORK

On the bus ride back to school, Finley closed her eyes and thought about *Invention #5*. She imagined herself skipping across the canvas, joining the playful colors in their game of tag. Red had just tagged her on the arm, and she was running after Blue with a brush in one hand and a palette in the other. She swerved and cornered Green at the edge of the painting. Suddenly Green leaped right off the canvas onto the museum floor. Finley took a deep breath and jumped.

When she landed, Finley was standing outside a museum. A huge crowd stood nearby. Everyone was dressed in black. She was wearing black, too — a black beret and a long, black trench coat.

The important-looking man from Olivia's boring horse portrait strutted up in a black suit and introduced Finley. The audience exploded in applause. Then the man pulled a cord, releasing a giant, black sheet of fabric that hung across the front of the museum. It tumbled down like a waterfall, exposing humungous, sparkly, rainbow letters that read: *FLOWERS MUSEUM OF ART.*

As classical music filled the air, Finley tugged off the sash around her waist, and let her coat fall. Her dazzling, rainbow-sequined outfit sparkled in the sun.

The crowd went crazy, cheering and throwing flowers at her feet. Then they tore off their own jackets and coats to reveal a sea of beautiful, brilliant colors! Finley caught sight of Mom, Dad, Zack, Evie, and Olivia. Dad waved, looking proud, and Mom blew kisses and wiped happy tears from her eyes.

But wait a minute, Finley thought, *where's Henry?*

At that moment, over the chatter of the crowd and the symphony's serenade, Finley heard another noise — an engine! She looked up just in time to see a biplane zoom overhead, pulling a long banner that read: *FLOWER POWER.*

Henry saluted her from the cockpit. Finley waved up at him as he did a loop de loop, then circled back again.

Just then, Henry's voice echoed in her ear. "Earth to Finley! We're here."

Finley opened her eyes and glanced around. The museum and crowd were gone, and so was her sparkly outfit. She was sitting on a bus full of noisy kids. There was a crick in her neck, and she'd drooled on her shirt. She wasn't a world-famous artist with her very own museum — yet.

"I must have fallen asleep," she said dreamily.

"Yep," said Henry. "All that art wore you out."

When they'd gotten back to the classroom and put away their things, Ms. Bird rang the chime. "Grab a seat, everyone!" she said. "I hope you all enjoyed visiting the museum. I can't wait to hear your thoughts. For your group project, you'll be discussing your favorite museum piece and giving a presentation that answers the very big question I mentioned earlier."

On the board in humungous letters, Ms. Bird wrote:

WHAT IS ART?

"Does it have to be a *group* project?" Olivia piped up. "What if I have my own idea?"

Ms. Bird smiled. "Then share it with your group! You have half an hour to brainstorm, so go ahead and get started."

Group work, shmoop work, Finley thought. But she grabbed her sketchbook and pulled a chair up to Olivia's desk.

"You go first," Henry told Olivia, "since you already have an idea."

Olivia sighed. "Fine. But you're not going to like it." She cleared her throat. "Art is beautiful. So we'll paint a beautiful still life with flowers and play some beautiful music to go with it." She looked at Finley and Henry expectantly.

"Hmm," said Henry.

"That's it?" said Finley.

"See?" said Olivia. "I knew you wouldn't like it."

"It's just that I don't think that answers the very big question," Henry said. "Because not all art is beautiful."

Olivia frowned. "Do you have a better idea?"

Henry made his thinking-hard face. "We could do portraits and talk about how art freezes a moment in time, like that painting of the girl under the tree."

"But what about *my* painting — *Invention #5*?" said Finley. "It showed the parts of art — lines and shapes and colors."

Olivia shook her head. "I *still* don't get why you like that one."

Just then, Ms. Bird came to check in on the group. "How's the brainstorming going?"

"Not so good," said Olivia. "They don't like my idea."

Finley shrugged. "Well, you don't like ours either."

"It's not that we don't like it," Henry told Olivia. "We just have our own ideas."

"Maybe we could divide up our twenty-five minutes and do three separate presentations," Finley suggested. "That way we could all do what we want. Problem solved!"

"Now, *that's* a good idea," said Olivia. "We'd have eight minutes and twenty seconds each."

Ms. Bird shook her head. "I'm afraid that won't work. That would be three individual projects. For a group art project, you have to work *together*."

Olivia sighed. "I guess we're stuck then."

"I guess so," said Finley.

* * *

Finley's group spent the rest of the afternoon brainstorming, but they still couldn't settle on an idea for their project.

"Maybe we can work on it after school tomorrow," Henry suggested. "I don't have soccer practice."

"Sure," Finley said. "We can meet at my house if you want."

Just before it was time to pack up for the day, Ms. Bird rang the chime. "Class, before we go, I want to explain today's homework — it's an art assignment, due tomorrow."

Finley turned her chair around and put on her listening ears.

"Sometimes artists use observation," Ms. Bird continued. "They look carefully at the world around them, like in the still-life paintings at the museum. Your homework for tonight is a fall harvest still life. Arrange some foods from your fridge and sketch them. After that, write a short poem to go with your drawing."

Suddenly, fireworks went off in Finley's head. *This could be my chance!* she thought. *I'll make something Fin-tastic, and everyone will love it. Then Henry and Olivia will listen to me!*

Chapter 7

MOLDY MASTERPIECE

When Finley got home from school, she cleared off the dining room table. She was already picturing her class gathering around to congratulate her on the still life and tell her what a great artist she was. She'd make a big splash and get Olivia and Henry to see her point of view at the same time. Mom and Dad would definitely reserve a spot on the fridge for her after that!

Finley got her craft box and took out some pencils and a piece of drawing paper. It was time to put her plan into action. "Hey, Mom," she called, "do we have a tablecloth? Maybe a lacy one that looks expensive and old?"

Mom was drifting from one room to the next, looking for her wallet. "I don't think so, honey," she said, poking her head through the doorway. "What's it for?"

"My fall still life. I want it to look fancy, like the ones we saw in the museum today."

"Could you use something else?" Mom asked. "Like a dishtowel?"

Finley frowned. "A dishtowel is *not* fancy."

Just then, Mom spotted her wallet in the basket of found things on the kitchen counter. "You'll have to look around, sweetie," she said, grabbing the wallet. "I've got to run — I'm late for book club." She kissed Finley's forehead and slung her bag over her shoulder. "Maybe Dad can help."

Finley sighed. If anyone was going to help her find something fancy, Dad was not that person. "What about fruits and veggies?" she asked. "Do we have anything colorful?"

Mom headed for the door. "Look in the fridge," she said over her shoulder. "There's not much, but I'm going shopping tomorrow."

Drat, thought Finley. *Tomorrow is too late. If it were Zack's homework, I bet she'd drop everything and go shopping today.*

Finley rummaged through the kitchen drawers. She found balls of rubber bands, chip clips, coupons, chopsticks, birthday candles, and millions of twist ties, but nothing that even resembled a lacy tablecloth.

Just then, Finley had a brilliant brainstorm — she could use Dad's paisley bathrobe! She grabbed it from the hook in his closet and spread it out across the dining room table so it looked artfully messy, like someone had just happened to throw it down.

Now for the fruits and veggies, Finley thought. She opened the fridge and peered inside. There was nothing fresh and colorful like in the still-life paintings at the museum. Just smelly, shriveled-up mushrooms, a couple of scraggly carrots, a bruised apple, some withered lettuce, and half of a sad-looking onion wrapped in plastic. They were all dingy and dull. And they didn't smell so great either.

Finley was about to give up when she unearthed a hunk of orange cheddar that had been hiding behind the hummus. It was crumbly and half-covered in blue-green mold. *At least it's got some color,* she thought.

Next she grabbed a couple of slices of bread and an almost-empty bottle of juice. She arranged everything on the bathrobe next to the crispy remains of Mom's African violet.

"Voilà," Finley muttered. *"Wilted Still Life with Dead Plant." It might not be pretty*, she thought. *But it's still. And it's life.*

At that moment, Evie bounded into the room. "Ooh!" she said, holding her nose. "What are you *doing*?"

"It's called a still life," said Finley. "It's for school."

"It looks pretty dead to me," said Evie. "Maybe it's a *zombie* still life!"

"Out!" said Finley, pointing to the door.

"*Okay.*" Evie scurried backward into the kitchen. "But don't say I didn't warn you . . ."

Finley walked around the table, surveying her still life from all angles. Something was missing, but she couldn't figure out what. Finally she gave up, grabbed her colored pencils, and took a seat. *All right*, she thought. *Time for some Fin-spiration.*

Finley sketched and shaded. She striped and swirled. Just as she was adding rainbow-colored rings to the onion, Zack came in and plunked his backpack down beside her.

"What is *that*?" he said, eyeing the strange arrangement.

"My homework." Finley said, coloring the bruise on the apple a brilliant blue. "It's a fall still life."

"Wow," Zack said. "That's one funky fall still life."

Finley glared at her brother. "Don't *you* have homework to do or something? Maybe a test to study for?"

"I was going to get a snack first," Zack said. "But I just lost my appetite."

Zack tromped upstairs, and Finley put down her pencil. *The problem with this fall still life is that there's nothing fall-ish about it*, she realized.

Suddenly, Finley had an idea. She dashed to the backyard and collected the best leaves she could find. Then she marched back to the dining room and stuck them between the other objects in her still life. *There,* she thought. *That adds some fall flavor!*

Finley had just finished drawing the leaves and was working on shading the neon-green mold on the cheese when Dad came out of the office.

"What is that smell?" he called from the kitchen.

"My still life!" Finley answered. "It stinks!"

"Come on," Dad said, poking his head through the dining room doorway. "It can't be that bad."

"No," Finley said. "I mean it actually smells."

Dad came a little closer. "Oh," he said, sniffing. "You're right. Don't we have anything you can draw that's less . . . ripe?"

"Nope," said Finley, shaking her head. "I'm making the best of what I've got."

"Well, I guess it shows nature in action," Dad said. "That's what happens when you leave things too long. You've got to eat them while you can. Seize the day, I always say!" He picked up the phone. "I'm going to order a pizza for dinner."

Seize the day! Finley's heart leaped. That gave her a great idea! She ran to her room and grabbed the glow-in-the-dark watch she'd gotten for her birthday. Then she stretched it out on the table so it dangled off the edge, just like the pocket watch in the still life at the museum.

Finley added the watch to her drawing, making sure to include the time — 5:21 p.m. Then she stood back to take a look. It was a still life, but it didn't look still. Colors zoomed and zipped across the paper! Lines wiggled and waved!

Fin-tastic! Finley thought. *This still life is sure to make a splash!*

Chapter 8
SEIZE THE CHEESE

After lunch the next day, Finley hurried back to her classroom. She took one last look at her drawing and practiced reading the poem she'd written the night before. This was her chance to shine, and she wanted to be ready.

Finally, Ms. Bird stood at the front of the room and rang the chime. "All right," she said, "it's time to share your homework." She glanced around the class. "Who would like to go first?"

Before Finley could raise her hand, Olivia's arm shot into the air. Ms. Bird nodded in her direction. "Olivia?"

Olivia walked to the front, unfolded a big, wooden easel, and draped some wispy fabric over it for decoration. When she set her drawing on the easel, a murmur went through the room. Delicately shaded fruits and vegetables rested on a flowery tablecloth, along with forks, patterned plates, and a pair of silver goblets. The apples, grapes, and pears were plump and round; the eggplants and peppers were smooth and shiny; the bread and cheese were broken into beautiful, artistic hunks.

Sheesh, Finley thought, *the inside of Olivia's fridge must look like a royal picnic.*

"This is my still life," Olivia announced, "inspired by the paintings at the museum. I tried to show the beauty of the fall harvest. My poem is entitled 'Feast':

Fancy forks and pretty plates —

A table set for two.

Pink and purple flowers

In a vase that's white and blue.

Yummy fruits and veggies

Are a feast for eyes to see —

A still life to remind us

Of how sweet life can be."

Olivia smiled primly as she finished.

Oh, for crying out sideways, Finley thought. *She doesn't even like fruits and veggies!*

"Thank you," said Ms. Bird. "That was just lovely."

The class clapped, and Olivia curtsied. She grabbed her drawing, folded up her fabric and easel, and sashayed back to her seat.

Finley hesitated. Now that she'd seen Olivia's still life, she wondered if hers would make a splash after all. She took a peek at her artwork's swirly, brilliant colors.

It's different, Finley told herself. *It's special.*

She decided to wait and go last. That way, she'd make a lasting impression.

Henry volunteered to go next. He'd drawn a still life of take-out containers. Some were stacked into towers, and others were lying on their sides with food spilling out.

"Are those spring rolls?" Will blurted out. "I love spring rolls!"

Henry nodded. "We had Thai food last night. My poem is a haiku. I called it 'Dinnertime' because that's what it's about.

Steaming boxes hold
Gifts of curry and noodles.
Please pass the soy sauce."

The class clapped as Henry finished. His cheeks turned pink as he rolled up his drawing and took his seat.

"Henry, your still life was so realistic," said Ms. Bird. "I think you've made us all hungry!"

One by one, the students showed their art and read their poems. When everyone else had finished, Finley marched to the front of the class and unfurled her drawing.

"Finley," said Ms. Bird, "can you tell us about your piece?"

"Well . . ." Finley paused and took a deep breath. "I gathered some things from the fridge and arranged them. Then I drew what I saw. I was worried because the still-life paintings at the museum looked fancy, and we didn't have anything fancy in our fridge. In fact, that right there is some *really* moldy cheese."

Finley glanced at Olivia, who made a face like she'd just taken a bite of it.

"But then I remembered that art isn't always beautiful," Finley continued. "So this is our dining room table on October 14 at 5:21 p.m. I put in the watch to show that time is passing, just like the paintings at the museum. I also added some color to make things more interesting and some leaves to make it more fall-ish."

Finley set the drawing down on Ms. Bird's desk and took out her sketchbook to read what she'd written. "My poem is called 'Seize the Cheese':

Life is short, so seize the cheese!
Be happy that you're in it.
Make the most of every day —
Don't miss a single minute.
Just like all this funky food,
I wouldn't want to waste it.
(I'm glad I made it into art
So I don't have to taste it!)"

When Finley was finished, Ms. Bird smiled. "Thank you, Finley. You didn't draw it *exactly* the way you saw it, but it was very interesting — and inspiring! I might have to go home and clean out my fridge tonight."

There was a trickle of applause and a wave of whispers as Finley took her seat. "So," she said to Henry, "what did you think of my still life?"

"It was a *moldy*, but a goodie," Henry said. "Get it?"

Finley didn't laugh. She could tell that Henry didn't really get her drawing. And neither did anyone else. *So much for my chance to shine*, she thought.

"Class, thank you for sharing your wonderful still-life artwork," Ms. Bird said. "You can take a ten-minute rest break, and then we'll move on to science."

As soon as Ms. Bird had finished, everyone crowded around Olivia and Henry to get a closer look at their drawings.

"Those spring rolls look so real!" Kate said to Henry.

"Yours belongs in the museum!" Lia told Olivia. "I bet you'll be famous one day!"

Finley stared at her moldy cheese and held back her tears. *The cheese stands alone*, she thought glumly. *I'll never be an artist. I'll never be the one people notice.*

Chapter 9
A VERY BIG IDEA

After the dismissal bell rang, Finley quietly gathered her things and slipped out the door. She didn't tell Ms. Bird to have a Fin-tastic night. She didn't wait for Henry so they could walk home together. She didn't notice the sunshine or the way-up-high clouds. And she didn't hear the leaves as they crunched under her feet.

When Finley got home, there was a big bowl of apples on the kitchen counter. Someone had gone shopping.

It figures, Finley thought, staring at the mound of fresh, glossy fruit.

Just then Zack bounded in through the back door with his soccer stuff on. "How'd it go with the stinky still life?" he asked, snatching an apple from the bowl.

"I don't want to talk about it," Finley muttered unhappily.

Zack shrugged. "Suit yourself."

Finley grabbed her backpack and slunk up to her room. She closed the door and flopped onto her bed. Then she took out her sketchbook and flipped to her drawing from the field trip. Her *Invention #5* didn't look anything like the painting in the museum.

It's no use, Finley thought. *I'll never be famous.* She glared at the sketch. Then she crumpled it up, aimed for the trash can, and missed.

Just then, there was a knock at the door.

"Anybody home?" Henry asked, opening it a crack and peering in.

"What are *you* doing here?" Finley asked.

"Looking for you. Your brother said to come on up." Henry scooped up the crumpled ball of paper and slam-dunked it into the trash. "Two points!"

Finley groaned.

"Where have you been?" Henry asked. "What's wrong?"

"What's wrong is that I want to be a famous artist, but no one appreciates my style," Finley said. "I should forget it and copy someone else's."

"No way," Henry said. "All those pieces we saw in the museum weren't there because they looked like someone else's. Artists do their own thing, even if other people don't always like it."

Finley sighed and looked away. "That's easy for you to say — everyone *loved* your still life. Olivia's, too."

"Speaking of Olivia, she's waiting downstairs," Henry said. "We were supposed to come over and work on our group project after school, remember?"

Finley shook her head. "You and Miss Perfect should just do the project without me. It'll be better that way."

Henry frowned. "Weren't *you* the one who said art is *fun*?"

Finley looked at Henry, and a tear slid down her cheek.

"Come on," Henry said. "It's a group project, and it's due in two days. We need you."

Finley sniffed and grabbed a tissue from the box by her bed. "We're never going to answer the very big question. We can't even agree on anything small."

Henry walked to the door. "Well, Olivia and I are here, so we might as well try."

Finley picked up her sketchbook and followed Henry downstairs. Olivia was waiting in the kitchen, where Evie was practicing her magic show.

"Hey," Evie said, "want to see some tricks?"

"Maybe later," said Finley. "Why don't you try them out on Mom first?"

"Okay," Evie said. She flung her cape over her shoulder and waved her wand in the air. "Close your eyes, and I'll disappear!"

Is that all I have to do? Finley thought. She closed her eyes and heard Evie dash into the living room. When she opened them, Olivia and Henry were looking at her.

"Where did *you* disappear to after school?" Olivia asked.

"Sorry," Finley said, taking a seat at the kitchen table. "I forgot we were meeting. I was too busy thinking about my failure of a still life."

"It was kind of . . . different," Olivia admitted. "But I wouldn't call it a *failure*."

Finley frowned. "It definitely wasn't a success."

Olivia looked at Henry. Henry looked at Finley. Finley looked out the window.

"Why don't we go outside?" Henry suggested. "Maybe the fresh air will help us get some fresh ideas."

Finley searched through the cupboards and grabbed some granola bars. Then they headed to the backyard.

"I want to sit in the hammock," said Olivia.

"Come on," Finley said. "There's room for three."

Finley, Henry, and Olivia all piled onto the hammock and leaned back to watch the clouds.

What is art? Finley wondered. The very big question was harder to answer than she'd thought.

"I wish we could do something really different," Finley said.

"Why can't we just use my idea?" Olivia whined. "That would be easy."

"Easy for *you*," said Henry.

Olivia rolled her eyes.

"Maybe in order to answer the very big question," said Finley, "we need a very big idea." She twined her fingers around the silky hammock rope.

"We could take the whole class on a very big field trip," Olivia suggested. "I've always wanted to go to Paris. *That* would be fun!"

"Sounds good to me," said Henry. "Just think of all that yummy food!"

"*Or* we could combine all our ideas into one," Finley said. "Something beautiful that captures a moment. Something different and *fun* . . ."

Just then the breeze blew, showering them with leaves. "Look what we caught," Henry said, picking some out of the hammock. "Little pieces of fall!"

Another gust sent a leaf sailing right into Finley's lap. "Hey," she said, twirling it by the stem. "I think I've got it!"

"What?" asked Olivia.

Finley's eyes widened. "A totally art-rageous idea!"

Chapter 10
UNBE-LEAF-ABLE

Finley, Henry, and Olivia didn't have much time to plan. But they divided up the work, and by Thursday, they were ready to present their project. That morning, Finley met Henry and Olivia in front of the school. "It's a great day to make some art!" she said. "Are you ready?"

Henry grinned. "Let's do this!"

Olivia patted her backpack. "I've got the fabric and yarn in here. And that magic wand and cape your sister lent us will be perfect!"

They stood on the school steps and looked out on the lawn. "That's going to be the best spot for our project," said Henry.

"Yep," said Olivia. "Right where everyone will see it."

When they got to the classroom, Ms. Bird greeted them at the door. "Go ahead and unpack your bags and take your seats," she said. "We're going to start the day with our presentations. That way we'll be done in time for recess."

"I think we should save ours for last," Olivia said to Finley and Henry. They both nodded in agreement.

Finley tried to pay attention as the other students shared their projects, but she was extra hoppity. Amelia, Frances, and Arpin recreated an ancient Greek mosaic they'd seen on the field trip. Kate, Lia, and Will demonstrated ten different art materials and made a landscape like their favorite one from the museum. Harper's group shared a book they'd made about the artist Mary Cassatt.

Finally, it was Finley's group's turn.

"All right, class," said Ms. Bird, "we have one more presentation — Finley, Henry, and Olivia."

Olivia turned off the lights and stood at the front of the class. Henry went to the back of the room and put on the cape. Then Olivia pressed a button on the remote control and a picture of a humungous flower painting came up on the white board.

"Some people might think that pretty isn't important," Olivia began, "but looking at pretty scenes and objects can make you feel good. Art can remind everyone that the world is beautiful. It can even make a tiny flower into a big deal. Isn't that an awesome blossom?"

Henry gave Finley a nod, and she put on some mysterious music. Then Henry walked down the center aisle waving Evie's magic wand. When he got to the front, he spun around. "Art is magical!" he said in a low voice. "It can take us back to a moment in history."

Olivia pressed the remote, and a slide of a still life came up on the board.

"Does this look familiar?" Henry asked. "It's a still life from hundreds of years ago, just like the ones we saw in the museum. Art captures a moment in time. Like Finley pointed out in her poem, it reminds us to 'seize the cheese' before it gets moldy. Remember how those still-life paintings included all that weird stuff? Bubbles pop, candles melt, minutes tick away on watches, and flowers fade. Time passes, but art keeps things, places, and people alive."

Finley turned on the lights. "Art isn't just about the artist or the subject," she said. "It's about the people looking at it, too. Our project involves participation — so follow me!"

Ms. Bird and the rest of the class followed Finley, Henry, and Olivia out to the front of the school.

"Today we're going to make some art outside," Finley explained. "And everyone is going to help! Don't worry, we'll show you how. First, find a partner. Then come get some of Olivia's netting and two pieces of yarn." Finley reached into Olivia's bag and pulled out some see-through fabric and yarn.

"Tie a piece of yarn around each end of the fabric, like this," Henry said, knotting the yarn and pulling it tight.

"Next, pick a pair of trees and stretch the fabric between them," Finley said as she and Henry demonstrated. "Make sure they're close enough for the fabric to hang down like a net. Then tie the yarn around each tree trunk to make a leaf hammock!"

Finley and Henry finished tying their hammock and stepped back. "The hammocks will catch the leaves as they fall from the trees," Finley explained.

"You can even gather some leaves off the ground and fill yours partway to give it a head start."

"But don't get in it!" Henry warned. "It's a *leaf* hammock, not a people hammock."

Students formed a line in front of Olivia to get their fabric, then wandered around the yard, picking out pairs of trees. They tied their hammocks high and low, near and far. Soon there were twelve of them, hanging like wispy cocoons in front of the school.

Olivia glanced around. "It's working!" she said to Finley. "They're beautiful!"

Henry grinned. "They're unbe-*leaf*-able!"

Suddenly, the wind blew, and a flurry of leaves fluttered down.

"We caught some!" Lia shouted, pointing to the leaves suspended in her netting.

"We did, too!" yelled Will.

Everyone started scooping up leaves. Soon the
hammocks were bulging, suspended like giant
seedpods all over the lawn.

"Look!" Finley said to Henry and Olivia. "A whole
herd of hammocks!"

"Hooray for hammocks!" Henry said, grabbing a handful of leaves and tossing them in the air.

Before long, someone started a game of freeze tag, and Lia and Kate got into a leaf fight with Will and Arpin.

"Class!" Ms. Bird called. "I know it's hard to stop, but we need to get to recess. Let's gather around so Finley, Henry, and Olivia can finish up."

Finley, Henry, and Olivia stood behind their hammock. "In closing," said Henry, "we just wanted to say that art is . . . art! It can make you pay attention to things and help you remember a moment, person, or place."

"It can be beautiful," said Olivia. "Or it can just *be*."

"There are so many different types of art and so many reasons people make it," said Henry. "We made a list, and it filled up five pages of my notebook!" He held up his notebook and flipped through the pages to prove it.

"At first we couldn't agree on what to do for our presentation," said Olivia. "We were brainstorming in Finley's hammock when she got the idea. It was inspired by a falling leaf and by that video we saw at the museum of that man who made art out of nature."

"It was Olivia's idea to sit in the hammock in the first place," said Finley. "She also thought of using the fabric. And Henry figured out how to hang it."

"Thanks for helping create our leaf hammocks!" said Henry.

"We made something beautiful *and* captured a moment in time *and* had fun doing it," said Finley. "We hope you had fun, too!"

"I like how this group project turned into a class project!" said Ms. Bird. "Let's get a class picture! Everybody squeeze in together. On the count of three . . ."

Finley glanced over at Henry and Olivia. "Ready?" she whispered, grasping the edge of the hammock.

"One . . ." Ms. Bird held the camera up. "Two . . . three!"

Finley, Henry, and Olivia shook the hammock, and leaves flew everywhere. They drifted down like confetti as the class clapped.

Ms. Bird snapped the picture. "Gotcha! Well done, everyone. That was quite the *Fin*-ale."

Chapter 11
TASTES LIKE FALL

That night at dinner, Evie plunked her plate down next to Finley's. "I saw your leaf hammocks in front of the school!" she said, helping herself to chips and salsa. "They were waving around like ghosts in the wind! I told Lucas they were tree spirits, and he got scared and told Mr. Green."

"*I* spotted them after soccer practice," Zack said. "You could see them from halfway down the block. They looked pretty awesome."

"That's our creative girl," Dad said, smiling proudly. "Always thinking up something interesting."

"*Fin*-teresting," Mom corrected.

Wow, Finley thought. *Maybe they do notice me after all.* "Thanks," she said. "We had fun making them — the whole class helped. And Ms. Bird told us that Principal Small is going to hang a picture of them in the hallway so people can still see our project after we take the hammocks down. She wanted to remind everyone that we can do big things when we work together. And she's going to throw us an art party tomorrow afternoon!"

"Lucky!" said Evie. "You get to do all the good stuff! All *we* do is coloring, and Mr. Green says you have to stay in the lines."

"Maybe we can make some leaf hammocks in the yard," Mom suggested. "Finley could show us how."

"Sure," Finley said. "I can ask Olivia where she got the fabric."

Zack nodded. "That'd be cool."

Suddenly Evie's eyes grew wide. "We could fill them with candy!" she shrieked. "Or put mummies in them for Halloween!"

Dad laughed. "Haunted hammocks! We'll have the best-decorated house in the neighborhood. We could even start a Halloween tradition."

"*This* mummy wouldn't mind an after-dinner rest," Mom said when they'd finished eating. "Anyone up for watching the sunset? It's so pretty out."

"Can we bring dessert?" Evie asked as Finley and Zack helped clear the table.

Mom smiled. "Why not?"

Dad cut up some slices of freshly baked pumpkin bread and grabbed a stack of plates and napkins. Then everyone followed him to the backyard. They crunched through the sea of leaves and headed for the hammock.

"Pretty soon it'll be raking time," Dad said.

Zack groaned. "Don't remind me."

"Up you go," Mom said, holding the hammock still so Evie could climb in.

Finley flopped down beside Evie, and Zack sat beside Finley. The sun was just sinking below the trees, casting a pinkish-orange glow on their faces and on the rows of feathery clouds that streaked the sky.

"Thanks for letting us use your cape and wand," Finley said to Evie. "They worked great for our presentation."

Evie stopped wiggling her loose tooth and grinned. "No problem. You let me borrow your stuff all the time."

Zack rested his foot on the ground and rocked the hammock gently. Finley leaned her head back and closed her eyes. She could hear the humming and honking of far-away traffic. There was a chill in the air, but with Zack and Evie on either side of her, she was warm. At that moment, being Finley-in-the-middle didn't feel so bad. In fact, it felt like she was right where she belonged.

"Here you go," Dad said, handing them each a plate of pumpkin bread. "It's a new recipe. Hope you like it."

Evie took a big bite. "I love it," she mumbled. "It tastes like cinnamon."

Finley broke off a piece and popped it into her mouth. It was still warm, and spicy-sweet. "*Mmm*," she said. "It tastes like fall."

Chapter 12
P-ART-Y!

The next day after lunch, Finley, Henry, and Olivia raced back to their classroom. All the desks had been pushed together into groups and covered with thick brown paper. Music was playing, and Ms. Bird's desk was draped with a checked tablecloth. Fruits, cheeses, and crackers were artfully arranged next to a pitcher of punch and stacks of paper plates and napkins.

"Woo-hoo!" Henry hollered. "Let's get this p-*art*-y started!"

Ms. Bird laughed. "All right," she said. "But first let me go over the activities." She paused as the class gathered around. "We have a drawing station with colored pencils and markers; a collage station with magazines and paper to cut and paste; a sculpture station with recycled plastic and cardboard, and masking tape and wire for building; and a painting station where you can mix your own colors and make your mark on the class canvas." She pointed to the back counter, where a huge piece of painting canvas had been unrolled and taped in place. "Choose your favorite activity, or try them all. There's also a snack station with an edible still life on my desk, so please help yourselves."

"Cool!" said Henry. "We can finally eat the still life!"

Ms. Bird smiled. "Let me know if you need any help," she said. "And don't forget the most important part — have fun!"

Finley, Henry, and Olivia went straight to the painting station. Finley got a big brush and squeezed some red and yellow paint onto her palette. She mixed them together, then added the tiniest bit of black. "Look," she said. "I made up my own color. I call it Fiery Fall."

Henry peered over Finley's shoulder. "I call it orange."

"It's a certain *type* of orange," said Finley. "My special color recipe."

Henry helped himself to yellow and blue. "My color's going to be Mantis Green," he said, "after my favorite bug."

"I want to mix my own signature color, too," said Olivia, reaching for the blue and red.

"Let me guess," said Henry, "Princess Purple?"

"No," said Olivia. "Perfect Plum."

Once Olivia had finished mixing, they took their palettes and brushes over to the big canvas. They made wavy lines and squiggles and dots.

"I have to admit, that does look pretty cool," said Olivia, "even though it's just colors."

Finley glanced around the room. Everywhere she looked, students were making stuff. Lia was building a castle out of toilet paper rolls and plastic bottles. Kate was cutting up magazines to make a collage. Will was working on a feathery sculpture that looked like a giant cat toy.

"What should we do now?" Finley asked.

"What about portraits?" Henry suggested, pointing to the drawing station.

"All right," said Olivia. "But let's make them good."

Finley and Henry got the clipboards, and Olivia passed them some paper. "We should try to show who we *really* are, not just the way we look," said Finley. "Like that painting of the girl at the museum."

Henry grabbed a pencil. "I'll do your portrait," he told Finley.

"I'll draw you," Finley told Olivia, "as long as you're not mad if it's not the most beautiful portrait."

"You can do it however you want," said Olivia. "Just try to include my new barrettes."

Finley grinned. "Deal."

"I'll do yours then," Olivia said to Henry.

"Prepare to be portrait-ed!" Henry announced. "Ready . . . set . . . draw!"

Finley studied Olivia's face. It was like she was seeing her for the first time — her wide, blue eyes, her silky bangs, the way the right corner of her mouth turned down just slightly when she was concentrating. Finley's marker danced across the page.

"Hold still!" said Henry. "You're drawing with your whole body!"

"I'm a person," Finley told him, "not a still life! I can't sit as still as an apple." She drew Olivia with swirly eyes, pink cheeks, curly hair, and rainbows coming out of her ears to show how she was always thinking. Then she added a wispy-fabric scarf and purple curls in Olivia's hair to match her barrettes.

"It's Fin-ished!" Finley announced, holding up her drawing.

"Whoa, that was fast!" said Henry. "It's really . . . colorful."

Finley nodded. "I tried to show her spunk."

"I have spunk?" Olivia asked.

"You've been spunk-ified!" said Henry.

Olivia examined the drawing. "It's not exactly my style," she said. "But it is pretty cool. Let's see yours, Henry."

Henry hesitated. "I'm still working on it — it's hard to capture the essence of Finley, especially when she won't hold still."

Finley tried not to move a muscle. But suddenly she had itches all over, screaming to be scratched. "Are you almost done? I can't stand sitting still. And my foot is asleep."

"Here's what I have so far." Henry turned the clipboard around so Finley could see.

"I like the way you did my hair," Finley said. "And there's not a freckle out of place!"

"Thanks," said Henry. "I gave you some chocolate chips to help you get ideas, and your pencil and sketchbook in case you get a brainstorm."

Finley laughed. "You thought of everything!"

Henry shook his head. "Something's still missing."

Finley wiggled her toes and made a face. "Yikes! My foot's waking up — it's all tingly and sparkly!"

Henry's eyes lit up. "That's it!" He grabbed some glitter glue and dotted and dripped it across his paper. Then he used his finger to smear it all around. "There," he said. "Olivia's spunk-ified, and you're sparkli-fied!"

"Awesome!" said Finley. "I'm shining!"

Henry held the drawing out to her. "You can keep it if you want."

"Thanks," Finley took it and offered hers to Olivia. "You can keep mine, too. What about yours?"

"Hold on a sec," Olivia said, squinting at her drawing. She added a few final lines, then set it down.

"Wow," said Henry. In the portrait, Henry was sitting under a tree, writing in his notebook. He was wearing his baseball cap and red high-top sneakers. Behind him were softly shaded clouds and smudgy layers of hills.

"I put you under a tree, just like that portrait you liked at the museum," Olivia explained. "You're making one of your lists. And there are some of your books beside you — a bug book and a cookbook."

"The sky is beautiful!" said Finley. "So is the tree — I wish I could climb it right now!"

Finley, Henry, and Olivia put their pictures side by side.

"They look good together!" said Olivia.

"Those are definitely not *bore*-traits," Henry joked.

Finley grinned. "I love making art! I still want to be an artist one day."

"You should," Olivia told her. "You're like an idea factory."

"More like an idea garden," said Henry. "You're always sprouting new thoughts."

"We all are," Finley said. She pointed out the window to the leaf hammocks swaying in the breeze. "Just look what we made together."

About the Author

Jessica Young grew up in Ontario, Canada. The same things make her happy now as when she was a kid: dancing, painting, music, digging in the dirt, picnics, reading, and writing. Like Finley Flowers, Jessica loves making stuff. When she was little, she wanted to be a tap-dancing flight attendant/veterinarian, but she's changed her mind! Jessica currently lives with her family in Nashville, Tennessee.

About the Illustrator

When Jessica Secheret was young, she had strange friends that were always with her: felt pens, colored pencils, brushes, and paint. After repainting all the walls in her house, her parents decided it was time for her to express her "talent" at an art school — the famous École Boulle in Paris. After several years at various architecture agencies, Jessica decided to give up squares, rulers, and compasses and dedicate her heart and soul to what she'd always loved — putting her own imagination on paper. Today, Jessica spends her time in her Paris studio, drawing for magazines and children's books in France and abroad.

Tastes-Like-Fall Pumpkin Bread

Get a grownup to help you make this spicy-sweet fall favorite! Be on the safe side — make sure to have an adult supervise and do the baking!

What You'll Need:

- 3 cups flour
- 2 teaspoons baking soda
- 1 teaspoon salt
- 2 teaspoons cinnamon
- 1 teaspoon nutmeg
- 1 teaspoon cloves
- 1 teaspoon allspice
- 1 (15-ounce) can of pumpkin
- 1 cup oil
- 2 ¼ cups sugar
- 4 large eggs

Note: Cinnamon can be used in place of any of the other spices if you don't have them. You can also add 1–2 cups chopped apples or chocolate chips for some Fin-teresting flavor!

What to Do:

1. Have an adult preheat the oven to 350 degrees.
2. Butter two large loaf pans or four small loaf pans.
3. Mix dry ingredients. Mix wet ingredients in a separate bowl. Mix dry ingredients with wet ingredients.
4. Spoon the batter into prepared pans, filling them about halfway.
5. Bake until the centers of the loaves spring back when pressed, about 40 minutes, depending on the size of your pans. (Have an adult check for you.)
6. Let cool for five minutes, then turn out the loaves onto a wire rack and let cool completely.

Fall Still Life

Make sure to ask an adult to help you find foods to draw!

What You'll Need:

- Foods from your kitchen, preferably fall fruits and veggies like apples, grapes, pears, squashes, pumpkins, and sweet potatoes — but other foods work, too!
- Leaves from outside, for a fall-ish feeling
- A piece of fabric, like a tablecloth, dishtowel, or blanket — or even a piece of clothing like a shirt
- Paper to draw on
- A pencil, and colored pencils, crayons, or markers if you want a splash of color

What to Do:

1. Drape the fabric over a table or chair — make sure to leave some wrinkles!
2. Arrange the foods and leaves on the fabric, with larger items at the back and smaller ones in front.
3. Starting with the objects closest to you, lightly sketch the contours — or outlines — of each

object, paying attention to their general shapes. Once you finish drawing the closest object, move on to the objects next to or behind it.

4. Add some details. Look for the shadows under, on, and between objects and shade them in with the side of your pencil.

5. Add some color if you want, layering your colored pencils, crayons, or markers.

Tip: Don't sit too close while you're sketching — it's easier to get a good perspective from a couple of feet away.

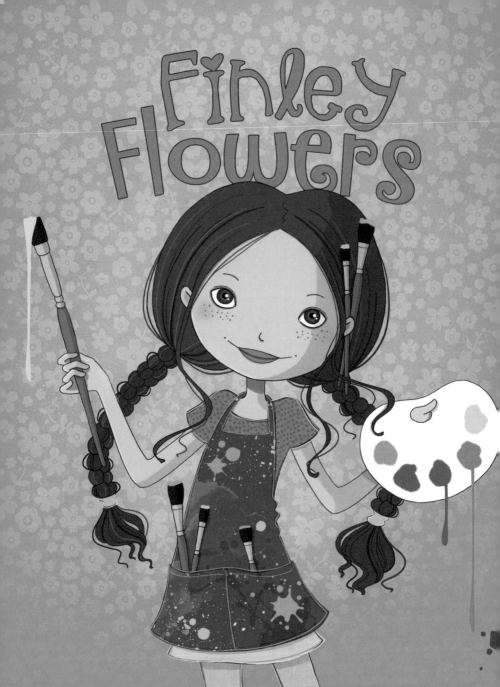

Be sure to check out all of Finley's creative, Fin-tastic adventures!